For Katie and Alice,
the gifts of my life
B. B.

For Janet and Angus

K. M. D.

Text copyright © 2017 by Bonny Becker
Illustrations copyright © 2017 by Kady MacDonald Denton

First edition 2017

Library of Congress Catalog Card Number pending
ISBN 978-0-7636-4923-4

17 18 19 20 21 22 TLF 10 9 8 7 6 5 4 3 2 1

Printed in Dongguan, Guangdong, China

This book was typeset in New Baskerville.
The illustrations were done in watercolor, ink, and gouache.

Candlewick Press
99 Dover Street
Somerville, Massachusetts 02144

visit us at www.candlewick.com

A Christmas for Bear

Bonny Becker

illustrated by

Kady MacDonald Denton

CANDLEWICK PRESS

Bear had never had a real Christmas.
He'd never had a tree with a sparkling star,
or candy canes, or even gingerbread bears.
But he'd read all about it.
Clearly, the most important thing was pickles.

One frosty night, Bear heard a tap, tap, tapping on his front door.

When he opened the door, there was Mouse,

small and gray and bright-eyed.

"Merry Christmas!" cried Mouse.

"Maybe," said Bear.

Bear had agreed to have a Christmas party. He'd never had one before.

"Do we open the presents first?" Mouse asked eagerly.

"Presents?" Bear shook his head. "Most unseemly."

"What!" Mouse's eyes opened wide. "No presents?"

"We shall sit around the tree and eat. I might even read a poem.
Surely that will do," Bear declared.

Then Bear went to the kitchen to get the Christmas pickles.

But when he came back . . . no Mouse!

"Mouse? Where are you?"

Mouse didn't answer.

Bear heard a tiny scurrying sound. It was coming from upstairs.

Bear climbed the stairs to his bedroom.

The scurry sound was under his bed!

"Mouse?"

"Yes?" came a muffled voice.

"Are you looking for a present?"

Mouse peeped out from under the bed; he had a bit of dust on his nose.

"Perhaps," said Mouse.

"Unnecessary hogwash!" Bear scolded. "We have pickles, remember."

"Oh," said Mouse.

   And Mouse trudged behind Bear back to the living room.

Bear went to the kitchen to get the cheese.

But when he got back to the living room . . . no Mouse!

"Mouse, you're looking for a present again, aren't you?"

"Maybe," came a tiny voice. It was out in the hall.

Bear opened the closet door.

There was Mouse. Small and gray and guilty-eyed.

"Not even one tiny present!" squeaked Mouse.

"The pickles are from France!"
declared Bear.

"But surely—" said Mouse.

"And furthermore," continued Bear, "I shall be reading a long and difficult poem."

Then Bear headed back to the kitchen to get the cookies, but before he got there, he quietly turned and tiptoed back to the living room. No Mouse! (Of course.)

"MOUSE!"

Mouse scampered out from behind the tree, tinsel dangling from one ear.

"PICKLES AND POEMS!" bellowed Bear. "THAT IS THE CHRISTMAS SPIRIT!"

"Yes, Bear," sighed Mouse.

Mouse sat in front of the crackling fire.

Bear served them pickles and cheese and cookies and tea

smelling of cinnamon and oranges. Bear nibbled and sipped.

Mouse did, too. But his tail was sad.

Bear cleared his throat. Mouse looked up.

"'Twas the night before Christmas," Bear pronounced.
"When all through the house,
not a creature was stirring,
not even a **mouse**."

Bear stared sternly at Mouse.

"The pickles are wonderful," whispered Mouse.

Bear continued.
"The **stockings** were hung by the **chimney** with care . . ."

Bear paused and glanced over at Mouse.

Mouse took a mournful bite of his pickle.

*"The **stockings** were hung by the **chimney** with care . . ."*

Bear repeated more loudly.

"THE STOCKINGS—"

Mouse leapt up, his eyes as bright as Christmas candles.

"You do have a present for me!" he cried, pointing at the mantel.

"You have stockings!"

"Certainly not! Impossible! Monstrous assumption!"

rumbled Bear, but he was smiling.

Mouse scrambled into his stocking
and popped back out with a package
wrapped in sparkling red paper.

Bear looked on eagerly as
Mouse tore off the wrapping.
"It is the best present ever," Bear
announced proudly. "Even if
it's not a pickle."

Inside was a shiny silver telescope!

Bear hurried Mouse out into the crisp winter night.

Mouse pointed the telescope toward the glowing moon.

"Most wonderful!" Mouse said softly. "Thank you, Bear."

"Yes, indeed." Bear smiled, then looked at Mouse. "Well?"

"What?" Mouse was busy studying the stars with his new telescope.

"Mouse? You didn't forget, did you?" Bear looked most stricken.

"Pickles and poems," said Mouse. Then he turned the telescope toward a nearby fir tree. "And presents!"

There, peeking out from the snowy branches, was a big red bow.

Bear hurried over and pulled out a wooden sled with shiny red runners.
"I've always wanted a sled with shiny red runners," said Bear. "Thank you,
Mouse. You are . . . " Bear swallowed. "You are an excellent companion.
Someone of whom I am most fond, a-a—"

"You are my best friend, too," said Mouse with a happy flick
of his whiskers. "Merry Christmas, Bear!"
"Merry Christmas, Mouse!" cried Bear.

Then Mouse and Bear jumped on the sled and swooped down
the hill under the shining stars of Christmas.